This Book Belongs To

- -

D1501141

Still I Shine

NIKKI ACE

ILLUSTRATED BY: Wesley Ace Jr. and Dani Ace

I am the sun –

the fireball in the sky you can't bounce.
I have a one-of-a-kind job:
I shine light in great amounts.

On earth, there is nothing more important than me - a glowing sphere that gives *life-giving* light, heat, and energy.

But not everyone is pleased
with the qualities I bring.
They try to block my sunshine
from eyes of all living things.

However, I can't be moved.
I am just so wonderfully divine.
Despite attempts to dim my light . . .

. . . still I shine.

One day a teensy weensy cloud
boldly floated to my front.
"Sun, get out of my way!" he yelled,
 followed by a wacky grunt.

He spread out his arms and legs
as far as they could stretch and stretch,

trying to cover my *glow* and *sparkle*
all the way from edge to edge.

To teensy weensy cloud I said,
"Nice to see you in front of me.
Now I can *use you* to provide shade
over the land and vast seas."

What this cloud meant for bad,
I quickly turned around for the good
to cool down hot sizzling weather
for plants and creatures livelihood.

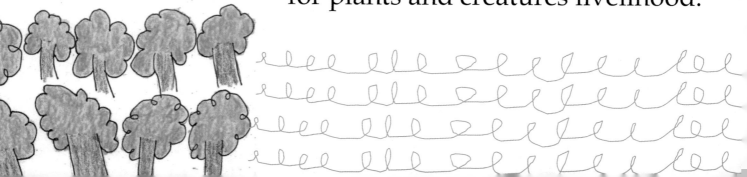

With my brilliance and my glimmer,
my razzle and dazzle that's all mine,
even with a teensy weensy cloud in front . . .

. . . still I shine.

So, this cloud got raging mad!
He started filling up
with vapor gas!
Bigger and bigger he became,
so heavy he cried out
tears of rain!

No longer could be seen from earth -
my beams of light go ablaze,
can't see my light that shines so bright

or my rays of light gleam and amaze!

So the cloud was pleased with glee.
He turned around in hopes I'd flee.
But he heard and saw with his own eyes,
me humming and singing . . .

"... still I shine."

Although unseen and out of view,
my light with rain helped plants to grow.
And what makes things even lovelier

is the colored, vibrant rainbow on show.

This was NOT his spiteful plan,
so he started showering a flurry of snow
in hopes the cold freezing temperatures

will take my sunny, *golden glow*.

Snow was no success for this cloud.
I was still there when he turned around.
So he settled for strong winds to blow and form
with fierce lightning and wild thunderstorms.

"Surely, now you'll go away and hide!"
moaned cloud with confidence and pride.
"My lightning and thunder will distract
all the attention your bright shine attracts."

With a "Woo Hoo!", "Yahoo!", and a "Yay Yay!"
cloud began to celebrate . . .
But I'm not leaving - I'm perfectly fine
and I whispered in cloud's ear . . .

"...still I shine."

Like a grumpy two year old child
having a tizzy on the ground,
cloud started having temper tantrums,
twisting in circles like merry-go-rounds.

He worked himself into a frenzy
as a tornado going BONKERS!
He was determined and so busy
to ensure my shine just would not conquer.

But he got tired and soon gave up.

He started to shrink and shrink and shrink.
As he slowly floated away,
he gasps . . . ponders . . . and deeply thinks.
Now with his squeaky lil' voice,
he expressed to me,
 "I have to admit, you are quite radiant.
Please accept my apology."

"Of course!" was my reply.
"We can work together next time!"
Then he disappeared in the sky
and as you guess . . .

...still I shine.

And just when you thought it was over,
darkness comes in to cover and block
my sunshine from creation on earth.
However, the moon just woke up!

The moon asked in a frantic voice,
"It's dark! What is there to do?
So many are lost . . . no one can see . . ."
I said, " I...CAN...USE...**YOU** !"

Having no light of her own,
the moon just did not understand.
But she trusted in my words,
with me, she'll be a helping hand.

I shined my sunlight on the moon.
She shed my sunlight on the earth.
You see, I can use anything for good:
Clouds, rain, and darkness have their worth.

So no matter *who, what, when,* and *where,*
or *whatever the time,*
even if it's hard to see me . . .